Character In The Book
KAETHE ZEMACH
Michael di Capua Books ◆ HarperCollins Publishers

For David
My partner from one page to the next

Once there was a Character who lived in a Book.
He had a nice life on the smooth, white pages.

The pages were filled with colorful pictures.
Some showed the Character in the Book growing up.

And some showed the Character having adventures,
like the time he made friends
with the monkeys in the jungle.

Or the time he sang with the dolphins and whales.

When the Character in the Book wasn't busy in a story,
he liked to bake cakes, play the trombone,
and work in his vegetable garden.

One day the Character in the Book
got a letter from his Auntie.
She was a character in a *different* book.

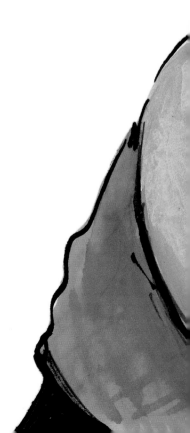

The Character in the Book was very excited.
As quick as he could, he got ready to go.
"I'm off to visit my dear beloved Auntie!"

"But first I'll have to find a way to get out of *my* book."

He tried to get out at the top of the page.

He tried to get out at the bottom of the page.

He thought about going backward,
but backward didn't make sense.
So the Character tried going forward . . .

and forward worked just fine!

He skipped and hopped and ran across the pages.

He whirled and twirled and spun across the pages.

He skated and scooted and pedaled across the pages.

He even tried riding an ostrich!

When he came to a river, he crossed the page in a boat.

And when a mountain stood in his way,
he found a tunnel and crawled straight through.

On and on went the Character in the Book,
until there were only a few pages left.

Then he stopped.

"Well, dear readers, I've almost come to the end of my book.
Thank you for keeping me company!"

And when the Character got to the very last page . . .
he jumped right out of his book!

"Goodbye!"